The Daydreamer Chronicles

TALES FROM REVERIE: MAYA

Jethro Punter

Email: jpunterwrites@gmail.com

www.facebook.com/thestairwayofdreams

https://daydreamerchroniclescom.wordpress.com/

*To everyone who has been there from the beginning,
whenever that was...*

CHAPTER 1

It was hot, hellishly so, and Maya was seriously regretting not bringing a bigger water bottle with her. Her throat was painfully dry and her mouth tasted of a mix of sand and spiral weed, neither of which were at all pleasant. She hadn't originally expected to be away for so long. The plan had been to take a quick look at the approaching Horror, staying no longer than absolutely necessary before sending her report to the rest of the Five. Unfortunately, circumstances had rather overtaken that initial idea, to the point at which she wasn't sure how, or even if, she would be able to make it back to the nearest village in one piece. Thirst was rapidly slipping down her list of immediate priorities, replaced by simply staying alive, which was now making a determined attempt at the number one spot.

With an inward groan of discomfort she flexed her shoulders which were starting to stiffen from her prolonged lack of movement, taking care not to raise herself above the protective camouflage of the undergrowth that currently sheltered her. Considering her size, just under six feet tall and rake thin, she was surprisingly good at not being seen when it suited her, and at the moment it suited her very well indeed.

Less than a dozen metres ahead of her there was a sharp cracking sound as the heavy, clawed foot of one of the passing Nightmares stamped down on a dry branch, shattering it like a dog biting through an old, brittle bone.

When she was younger the sudden loud noise would almost certainly have made her jump or at least give an involuntary gasp. She had been a particularly nervous child, partly as a result of her rather unsettled upbringing, which had led to the other kids in her village taking great pleasure in scaring or startling her whenever they could. However, years of experience and an unflinching determination to face her weaknesses head-on had changed Maya beyond recognition. A body that had once been gangly and awkward had evolved into something much more focused. Her tall, slim frame now gave the impression of a machine that had been refined and trimmed down over time into something completely functional, every surplus movement rejected.

So, rather than react in any way, Maya just lay completely still, one slow and perfectly measured breath in, one equally slow breath out, so gentle that the leaves of the plant directly in front of her face hardly moved. A Googly Bug was perched on the nearest stem and peered up at her short-sightedly, it's giant, multi-faceted eyes unfortunately as useless at focusing on something right in front of its face as they were amazing for spotting predators in its peripheral vision. As a result, most of its natural predators had eventually developed the ability to hunt the bugs by walking, slithering or flapping slowly and directly at them, leaving the Googly population sadly depleted. Maya supposed she should feel lucky to see such a rare inhabitant of Reverie up close, but at the moment she had much bigger and more immediate issues to hold her attention.

It had been just over a week ago when she had been sent out by the Five to investigate rumours that a new Horror had been seen out on the far edges of Reverie, right on the ragged western fringes of civilisation. While there were still the occasional scattered homesteads and even one or two villages out here, the inhabitants kept themselves very much to themselves, far removed from the hustle, the bustle and more importantly, the politics of the cities. The latest hot news stories from Nocturne, which would normally have run their course and cooled to mild disinterest within the day, would reach the residents of these remote settlements days or even weeks later, where they would briefly be the topic of muttered, scandalised conversation. Generally, the purpose of these chats would be to express a complete lack of surprise at the latest ridiculous shenanigans that the 'city folk' were getting up to and an associated shared thankfulness that they lived far away from such madness.

These exchanges were all too familiar to Maya, with the early years of her life having been spent in a small settlement extremely similar to those she had been trekking through over the last few days. Her family had been farmers, although describing them that way made them sound infinitely more successful and wealthy than the reality of the rather grim existence they had scratched out for themselves. There was a reason that civilisation only sat loosely on the land, like a dust cloth which might be pulled clear at any moment, and that reason was that the land itself was largely rock, dust, scrubland, and heat.

Maya's family had been one of the more recent arrivals in the area, ending up in a small settlement known as Perfidy, and as a result they been relegated to one of the very worst patches of land to farm, right at the end of the rickety, leaky pipeline that trickled desperately needed water from the half-hearted centre of the village to the outlying farmsteads. The whole place was a series of concentric rings of increasing misfortune. The richest and most successful lived near the centre, where they also enjoyed the best water supply, with the quality of life decreasing the further from the centre you lived. By the time the pipeline reached Maya's family, they were lucky to get anything more than a dribble of stained liquid, which only the most optimistic would describe as water. Despite this, her parents had been charged a small fortune by Cornelius Tutch, the ever-smiling businessman and self-proclaimed Mayor who had set up the water supply in the first place.

Living on the very outskirts of Perfidy, which was itself perched precariously on the edge of the civilised world, had meant that Maya and her family were right at the bottom of pretty much any social ladder, and the other kids in the area hadn't wasted any time letting her know it. The worst of them had been Cornelius Tutch's only daughter, Lottie, a hugely spoiled little princess who had inherited her father's superior smile but none of his genius for invention or engineering. Day after day she had taken every chance to remind Maya of her family's lowly status, fanning her nose theatrically every time Maya went near her and her clique of sycophantic friends.

"Phew... maybe you should use some of my father's water to wash yourself rather than grow those awful crops," she would drawl, as her friends tittered and giggled mindlessly in the background. After a few weeks, Maya had snapped and thrown herself at Lottie in a red mist of embarrassed fury, barrelling past Lottie's shocked friends and planting her firmly into a pile of muck that lay by the side of the dusty street.

It had made her heart sing to see Lottie sat despondently by the roadside, trying unsuccessfully to scrape mud and debris from her long, blonde hair, for once looking and smelling worse than Maya ever had, but that temporary feeling of elation had been punctured as soon as she had got back to the shack that her family called home and found that their water supply had been cut off completely.

She'd realised almost immediately why this was, but it had still taken her a long and restlessly guilty night to summon enough courage to admit to her parents what had happened. They were both good people, worn down by the toughness of life but with a hard pride in the centre of it all that was impossible to erode. So they didn't shout at her or scold her, just nodded, gave her a hug and set about their daily tasks, although now with the additional long trek into town to carry back a few of buckets of water at a time.

After a couple of days Maya hadn't been able to face the exhausted look on her father's face when he trudged back to their farm late in the evening, and the following morning she had gone to find Lottie and begged her forgiveness. It had been a horrible, soul-crushing experience and she had found it almost impossibly hard to swallow her pride in the face of Lottie's sneering and simpering superiority, her words of apology catching in her throat like lumps of cold porridge, but Lottie had eventually relented, and the next day the water had returned to its former pathetic trickle.

CHAPTER 2

It hadn't come as much of a surprise to her parents that when Maya had been old enough to leave and make her way to the city she had jumped at the chance, desperate to escape the tiny, cramped world she had been brought up in.

More than anything she wanted to see, hear and taste everything that Nocturne had to offer, although it hadn't taken long to realise that it wasn't going to be quite the fairy-tale she had dreamt of. The city turned out to be much dirtier and more crowded than she had expected, but she had stuck with it, the lively street-side cafés and market stalls capturing her imagination despite the surrounding grime.

To start off with she had also been amazed by the sheer number and variety of dreamers (and their accompanying Nightmares) that seemed to coexist with the inhabitants of the city, weaving their tiny, personal stories between the day to day activities of Nocturne seamlessly, often completely ignored. To see a dreamer was a relatively rare occurrence in the barren plains of the West, where the only dreamers you would find were those completely alone, no pursuing Nightmares, no adventures, just the occasional lonely looking individual surrounding themselves in the nothingness that the far reaches of Reverie offered.

She had watched in delight as a young boy was pursued by a monstrous ice-cream or an elderly woman made a slow but determined escape from a giant pair of snapping false teeth, amazed that no one else seemed to be as fascinated by these sights. But as is the sad case with every wonder in life eventually they became nothing more than background noise, generally ignored in favour of more immediate priorities or concerns.

She had worked incredibly hard to build a new life for herself, alternating between running errands down in the docks during the day and helping out at one of the cafés or bars in the evenings. The pay had been terrible, and the work down in the docks had increasingly led her to question her choices, with more than a reasonable share of the people she dealt with being at best shady, and at worst obviously criminal.

She had lodged in an attic room above one of the cafés where she worked, which cost her more than she got paid for her evening's employment, and which was hardly fit for habitation. Gaps in the slate roof let through rain, snow and a constant whistling breeze that kept her awake night after night until she finally became used to it, so tired she could sleep through the discomfort and noise.

Every now and then she would make the long journey home, catching a lift on a passing barge as far as the Weave would take her, then walking the last few miles to the edge of Perfidy. Somehow her parents always seemed to know she was coming, and by the time she reached their ramshackle home there would be food on the table and a kettle boiling away on the stove.

Although things had initially been a little strained, they soon settled into a comfortable pattern that fitted her new life. Every few months she would visit, staying for a couple of days helping out around the farm and sharing all the latest news about her life in the city, (which she was always careful to make sound more glamorous and successful than the rather shabby reality), before making the long journey back to Nocturne.

This had gone on for nearly three years, and although it was not the ideal life that Maya had dreamed of, it was comfortable, a routine that she could live with happily enough. Then everything changed, every aspect of the life she had known and left behind taken away in an instant.

CHAPTER 3

'Crack'... Maya's thoughts were dragged unwillingly back to the present as another Nightmare creature stamped its way past her. By this point she had lost count of how many had passed by her hiding place, but it was far, far more than she would ever have expected.

When she had been asked to investigate the appearance of another Horror, that was all she had expected to find. Horrors in themselves had the potential to wreak incredible havoc, spreading chaos and destruction wherever they went, but it was always something random and mindless, a whirling mess of dark dreams that would tear through anything unfortunate enough to get in its way, without any particular purpose or direction. This time was different though, there was something very unusual and very, very wrong, about this one.

For a start, the Horror didn't appear to be deviating from its route. It had been travelling in a completely straight line ever since Maya had first seen it, which in itself was completely unheard of. Secondly, and even more worrying, was the fact that this Horror appeared to have an honour guard of Nightmares accompanying it, marching grimly to either side.

The whirling darkness at the very centre of it all was still several hundred metres from where Maya had hidden herself, but even at this distance she could feel its effects, waves of misery and confusion spreading out in all directions, mixed in with choppy uneven currents in the air, disrupted by its passing. The increasingly strong sensations of despondency had a sharp edge, almost physically painful. Even though she was pretty sure it wasn't possible, every inward breath Maya took felt like she was breathing in a thick swampy fog, clogging her throat and lungs. Without thinking she took in a deeper breath than she intended, and despite her best efforts she was unable to stop a sharp cough escaping. Ducking even lower amongst the surrounding undergrowth she pressed her face as close to the ground as she could, but it was too late. The nearest group of Nightmares had stopped their slow march and turned to face the area where she was hidden, sniffing the air suspiciously.

Silently cursing her traitorous body for having let her down, and her equally traitorous mind for drifting away at such an important moment, Maya started to worm her way backward, but it was impossible to make anything other than very slow progress without giving her position away completely. The nearest Nightmares were now only a matter of metres away, heavy feet trampling the nearby plants underfoot, startling the previously peacefully resting Googly Bug enough for it to buzz away, its tiny wings hammering away faster than Maya could see, dragging it's disproportionate, massive-eyed head with it.

By now it was too risky to continue her slow retreat, with any movement likely to give her position away. Rummaging in the bag strapped to her hip Maya pulled out one of the packets of herbs that Grimble had given her before she departed, the pungent smell of aniseed drifting up and tickling her nose. She knew with an unpleasant certainty that this wouldn't be enough to save her, there were far too many Nightmares for that, but at least she would go down fighting, or if she was really lucky, perhaps buy herself enough time to make a break for the thicker forested area at the edge of the valley.

Rolling onto her back as quietly as she could she held the bag in her left hand and prepared to light the short fuse that would ignite the herbs, releasing a thick smoke that would at least slow the nearest Nightmares for a while.

Just as she was about the flick the stubby flint held in her other hand, tensing herself to run as far and as fast as she could before the herbs burned out, Maya saw the nearest Nightmares suddenly turn away from where she was hidden, cries of confusion coming from a variety of jaws, beaks, and snouts.

Across the valley, something was happening to the Horror. The centre of it was rippling queasily, and then without any further warning, a glowing shape burst from the very centre of the dark mass, ragged edges closing behind it, sealing the Horror closed again like a rapidly healing wound. At this distance it wasn't possible to make out any detail, the light blooming around the shape giving it a blurred, wavering outline, but whatever the figure was, it was moving extremely fast. Several of the closest Nightmares tried to get in its way, large clumsy limbs flailing awkwardly.

The first couple that tried immediately regretted their attempts. Whenever they made contact with the luminescent shape dashing through their ranks there was a bright, sparking impact and the Nightmares, despite their much larger size, were sent spin-wheeling through the air, landing heavily scores of metres away in crumpled, groaning heaps.

With growing concern, Maya realised that the pursuit was heading directly towards her hiding place, the glowing figure now close enough to make out more detail. It appeared to be a woman, putting Maya briefly in mind of the Lady, the dream being that had sent her out here in the first place, but as the uneven chase drew closer the differences became more obvious.

The Lady was made entirely of dream energy, reflected in her ever-changing and glowing form, whereas the woman sprinting towards her appeared to be just that, a woman but one who was completely surrounded by a glowing aura, flickering around her like a white-hot flame.

Realising that the chase was going to reach her whether she wanted it to or not, making a snap judgement that anyone being chased by the Nightmares was pretty likely to be someone she should side with, and frankly not being left with much other choice, Maya stood up from her hiding place and heaved the newly lit bag of herbs into the closest group of monsters. As it hit the ground the short fuse burnt out and the package sputtered into life, spraying a dark cloud of strongly smelling smoke in all directions. The Nightmares nearest to the smoke stopped dead in their tracks, frozen in place, flickering slightly like stuck frames in an old movie. Then one by one they came apart, dissipating into smoke themselves before vanishing completely with a variety of despairing wails, moans, and grunts.

By now the glowing woman had reached Maya, skidding to a halt just in front of her, and to Maya's surprise there was a spark of recognition in the woman's eyes as she looked across.

"You... you are from the Five. Lucid said that someone would come,"

Not really sure how to respond, Maya just nodded dumbly. She had never been very good at dealing with people, which was one of the reasons why her life now, out on the road and alone most of the time, was one that suited her so well. Although she doubted even the most confident and sociably capable of people would manage to handle a conversation out of the blue with a glowing woman who had just burst from the heart of a giant Nightmare.

To add to her confusion, she couldn't shake the feeling that the woman was someone she recognised, although she couldn't think where from.

"Tell Lucid I tried... but I wasn't able to stop it..."

The woman stopped for a moment, turning to fend off a Nightmare who had made it through the thinning smoke largely unscathed, a ball of light wrapping the Nightmare up tightly before a dismissive wave of the stranger's hand sent it ricocheting off into the distance, like a particularly ugly, angry rubber ball.

"You must warn them, tell Lucid, tell them all," the woman panted, keeping one arm outstretched, light radiating from her fingertips. "This Horror is different, someone created it... they made it to do something terrible."

"What do you mean... what will it do?" Maya managed to ask, but before the woman could answer they were disturbed by the unwelcome arrival of several more Nightmares which materialised almost directly beside them, bypassing the smoke completely.

The first of the creatures to appear was in the form of a giant spider, long legs skittering unevenly as it span into existence. Taking advantage of its momentary disorientation Maya ducked back out of its reach. "Why spiders," she muttered to herself, "I really, really hate spiders."

With a casual flick of her hand the woman sent the spider flying through the air, where it hit a nearby tree with a painful sounding crunch, before dropping to the ground and lying stunned on its back.

The spectacle of the giant creature flat on its back, with its long, hairy limbs twitching, didn't make it any less horrific, the sight of it still giving Maya the creeps. It was almost enough to completely distract her from the rest of the battle now raging around her, but years of finely honing her instincts and reflexes (and admittedly a reasonable amount of luck), meant that Maya rolled to one side just before a huge, twisted arm swung through the space she had been occupying just seconds before.

"Who or what in the Great Dream are you?" Maya panted as she sprang back onto her feet. "How are you doing..." she waved her hands, managing a surprising accurate mime of flinging one of the spiders through the air, "...whatever you are doing?"

Despite their precarious position the woman managed a smile, although it was through gritted teeth, and waved her hand in the direction of the Nightmare who had just tried to take Maya's head off. With a surprised and most un-nightmarish yelp the creature span through the air and landed awkwardly on several of its comrades.

"It's a long story... and not one we have time for now. But I know the Five from before your time... even if they don't talk about me anymore. The important thing is that we stop this Horror before it's too late."

The woman ducked as another Nightmare, this one looking like a terrible reimagining of a child's teddy bear, (if the child liked its bears to be at least eight feet tall with glowing eyes and far, far too many teeth), charged heavily towards them. It's clumsy attempts to grab her failed completely, furry arms grasping at empty air, before she rose back to her feet blasting the unfortunate teddy dozens of feet into the air with a sudden geyser that burst from the ground without warning.

"It's heading for the... Stairway," she told Maya, between heavy breaths. "They want to destroy the it."

"But that's so far away, it will never get that far. No Horror has ever..."

The woman laughed, a far more bitter sound than the laughter lines around her mouth would have suggested. Her breathing was becoming heavier, more laboured, and Maya noticed that the light that flickered around her was fading slightly. It seemed that whatever she was doing, while very impressive, was also taking its toll on her.

"This is not a normal Horror. I told you... it's special... tell Lucid, he will know what to do."

There was an unpleasant sucking sound and several more patches of darkness blinked into existence all around them, each one turning into a new Nightmare. The woman grimaced and the glow around her intensified again slightly, then she thrust her arms into the ground, a minor earthquake spreading out from where she was stood, toppling the newly arrived creatures like dominos.

"Go... run!" the Woman shouted, her eyes squeezed close in concentration.

Maya was caught in a brief moment of indecision, not wanting to leave the side of this strange arrival. Although they had only just met, she felt a strange connection, impossible to explain, that made the thought of leaving the woman to her fate almost unbearable. However, it was also clear that they were both running out of time. Despite the mysterious woman's incredible powers, more and more Nightmares were now converging on them, and the light that surrounded her was beginning to flicker unevenly, like a bulb nearing the end of its life.

Then in the middle of the mass of monsters a further figure appeared, that of a tall, blonde man striding confidently, looking completely at home amongst the surrounding creatures.

"There you are... I've been looking for you."

He had a deep, cultured voice that Maya would have found pleasant in other circumstances, but the fact that he was surrounded by Nightmare monsters that were respectfully stepping (or crawling, or flapping) out of his way made it pretty clear that he commanded these creatures and was not the friendly character that the broad smile on his face might suggest.

When the woman turned back to Maya, hissing "you need to go... now!" there was an unmistakable hint of fear in her eyes as they flicked back and forth between Maya and the new arrival.

For a moment the woman closed one hand protectively over the other and Maya could see that the light that surrounded her seemed strongest around a cheap and gaudy looking ring on the little finger of her right hand. Then the woman drew her hands apart with a deep inward breath before clapping them back together. A wall of light sprang up between her and Maya, slicing through the mixture of smoke and shadows that surrounded them like a knife, cutting Maya off from the conflict completely.

Although she could no longer see the battle, Maya could still hear the cries and roars of the Nightmares, which become increasingly loud and urgent. Then, with a suddenness that caught Maya out completely, the ring that she had seen only moments before on the mysterious woman's finger came arcing through the air, bouncing once off a nearby rock and skittering across the scrubby ground. The gem that topped the ring was still surrounded by a slight aura, and Maya felt an overwhelming compulsion to run across and pick it up. But before she could gather her thoughts or get anywhere near it, a murky patch of shadow formed around the ring. The last of the light surrounding it was completely snuffed out, and in the background she could hear the blonde man laughing triumphantly. At the same time the wall of light that had separated her from the Nightmares wavered and started to fragment, and Maya knew the glowing woman had been overwhelmed... or worse.

Then she was running, feet racing over the uneven ground with her previous immobility finally banished, giving way to a mindless adrenaline-fuelled sprint. The only route still open to her meant that she would be passing dangerously close to the Horror itself, but she had no other choice and each lengthy stride took her closer to its grim influence. She tried to concentrate her mind, to calm herself. Everything she knew about Horrors, everything that she had been taught, was that the negative dream energy that formed it would spill out and play tricks with her mind, and the closer she drew to it, the more she understood the truth of those warnings.

As she reached the ill-defined boundary between her world and whatever it was that made up the Horror itself, passing within a dozen metres of its grimly spinning base, she struggled to keep her footing as she was buffeted by the gusts of despair radiating from it. Difficult as it was to keep moving, the mental effects of being so close to the Horror were much worse. Her mind was almost overwhelmed by terrible images, bad dreams brought to life.

She knew that the visions that were rushing unwanted through her mind were just that, nothing more than fragmented snatches of memory that she had tried her best to bury, but that didn't stop her from shuddering as she was bombarded with misery after misery. Then one final, huge recollection hit her, the sight of the dark whirlwind so close making it almost inevitable, and Maya's thoughts jumped back five years, to when she had first experienced the effects of a Horror.

CHAPTER 4 – FIVE YEARS AGO

Maya had been away from home longer than normal, her last couple of jobs in Nocturne having been both more complicated and considerably more time consuming than expected. Unfortunately, her pay packets had remained disappointingly low, hardly reflecting the increasingly questionable and dangerous nature of the work she was being asked to carry out. Still, despite this she had managed to scrape together a bit more money than normal, making up for the paltry wages that she earned per job by accepting every single piece of work available.

Now she had a small bag filled with Threads, jingling quietly where she had stashed it safely in her pocket. She also had a couple of new scars and a painful pulled muscle in her shoulder, but for the moment she decided to forget about how she had earned the money and concentrate instead on what she would do with it. Although it hardly classed as a fortune, she was pretty sure that she had saved enough to pay for the most urgent of the repairs that her parent's farm so desperately and obviously needed, and which they stubbornly refused to mention or acknowledge whenever she visited.

As normal she had journeyed back to the edge of Perfidy on one of the Sornette barges, making its regular trading run between the city and the rag-tag cluster of villages and homesteads on the Western fringes of Reverie. On their outbound journey the barges would carry all sorts of cheap but fancy-looking trinkets, knick-knacks, and oddities from the artisans and workshops of Nocturne. There were cases packed with dresses and suits, top hats and walking canes, clockwork oddities and swirling snow-globes, all of which were in great demand with the wealthier and more upwardly mobile residents of the outlying lands. Then on their return journey the traders would take sacks of the mixed grains that grew in the sandy soils of the West, along with smaller consignments of dried herbs and plants, highly valued for their medicinal properties by the chemists and pharmacists back in Nocturne. It was an uneven trade, with weeks-worth of toil in the unforgiving ground exchanged for baubles and toys produced in bulk in the city, but one that seemed to work for everyone involved, especially the traders who shuttled eagerly between the two groups.

This barge, the 'Merry Dancer' was operated by a genial, although slightly pompous, old Sornette who went by the name of Kippler. He had been running the route between Nocturne and Perfidy for the last couple of years and during that time Maya had seen his barge and his waistline expand in line with his increasing wealth.

Unusually for a Sornette he had cultivated, at great effort, a long and greying beard which was threaded with beads and fine, glistening chains of silver and gold, taking the regular Sornette fascination with decorating their clothing to the next level. Kippler was immensely proud of this and would constantly stroke the hairs of his beard or toy with one of the fancy beads as he spoke, drawing as much attention to it as he could without actually pointing at his own face and shouting, "Admire my beard, it was really expensive!" Maya hadn't the heart to tell him that there were crumbs of his dinner caught up in the filigree, which made his chin look more like a picnic gone badly wrong than a work of art.

Still, Kippler was pleasant enough company, and Maya had travelled the route with him enough times to consider him, if not a friend, at least an acquaintance that she could happily pass time with swapping stories. He would tell her of his adventurous youth, working on the more dangerous trading routes as a general dogsbody for more successful merchants until he had raised the funds to buy his own vessel. In return she would share stories of her latest jobs, picked up down in the docks. She generally tried to skirt over the more criminal sounding things that she had found herself involved in, but Kippler was a canny old codger behind the bluster and pomposity, and he could generally read between the lines, picking out the pieces of her stories that she tried to hide away.

"You should watch out for Granny," Kippler told her solemnly, as she finished recounting her most recent exploits. "I don't know quite how she manages it, but even when you do a job for her, nine times out of ten you still come out of it owing her for the privilege."

"It's fine, don't be such an old fuss-pot, I can handle myself... and Granny too if needed," Maya laughed. "It's just work. Besides, she pays well enough and I've shown her that she can trust me. Sooner or later all of my efforts will pay off and she will let me have a chance at the real big money jobs."

"Still, you be careful young lady," Kippler was smiling as he spoke, but his words were steady and serious. "There is a reason that Granny has been running the docks for such a long time. Remember it's not always the cream that rises to the top..."

Maya gave him a reassuring pat on the shoulder, then absentmindedly brushed a couple of stray bits of lunch from his beard, which had been bothering her more than she had cared to admit to herself.

"I'm always careful, it's why I'm so good at what I do."

Kippler didn't question her any further, but it was clear that he was still worried, even though he didn't say as much out loud.

Although she would never admit it, even to herself, deep down Maya knew he was right. In her desperate race to gather as much money as she could, she had found herself getting sucked into lines of work she never would have even considered just a few months ago, and at the centre of everything that kept her awake at night, questioning what she had done the day before, was the gnarled, giggling figure of Granny. Sighing softly to herself, she resolved that things would be different when she returned to Nocturne.

The remainder of the journey passed quickly, but even that short time was difficult for Maya. She could hardly wait to see her parents and hand over the Threads she had carefully been hoarding for the last few months. She was pretty sure that it was going to be a bit of a battle to get them to accept her gift, but she was also sure that it would be well worth it, and had spent hours going over the arguments in her head.

"That's odd."

Kippler was looking off into the distance, pointing beyond the small jetty where they would shortly dock. Normally there would be a cart waiting to meet them and carry his goods the last few miles to Perfidy, but the jetty was deserted, with no one to be seen.

Maya hadn't quite reached the spot where Kippler was standing when she saw him suddenly stiffen, starting to rummage frantically in the various inside pockets of his long jacket.

"What is it?"

But Kippler just shushed her with an impatient flap of his hand without looking around. He'd managed to find what he had been searching for, a small but expensive-looking brass eyeglass which he was now staring intently through, mumbling something under his breath.

"What is it? she asked again. "What are you looking at."

This time Kippler did turn to face her, although Maya almost wished he hadn't. The colour had drained from his skin, other than under his eyes where the bags appeared even darker and heavier than normal. Without saying anything he handed her the eyeglass and holding her by the shoulders gently turned her on the spot until she was looking in the direction he intended.

Initially, Maya hadn't realised what she was looking at. There above the nearest ridgeline was a distant blurry shape, dark and foreboding, rising into the sky and lazily snaking its way across the horizon. The darkness of the twisting shape stark against the gentle red of the setting sun.

"Is that...?" Maya began, stopping as Kippler gave her shoulder a comforting squeeze.

"A Horror..." Kippler concluded for her, his voice tremulous, sounding his age for once. "It's a Horror. I hoped I would never see one again."

All Maya had been able to focus on was the dark stain against the skyline. Although it was impossible at this distance, she felt like the Horror was draining every bit of hope and optimism from her body, turning her bones to an ice-cold jelly.

The rest of the journey had passed in a blur, just remembered snippets, thin slices of terror with only darkness between. There had been the bump of the 'Merry Dancer' as it hit the jetty, Kippler's shouts behind her fading into the distance, and the unsteady helter-skelter run from the docks towards Perfidy.

The next thing she remembered was her panicked arrival at the edge of the town. Everywhere she passed through had changed beyond recognition and all much for the worse. Perfidy was a complete wreck, a deep ridge was carved through the town, buildings ripped open like tin cans, contents spilling across the street. In the very centre she had seen Lottie, staggering around blindly, completely unaware of her surroundings, calling out for her father. Despite her panicked concern for her own family Maya had stopped for a moment and tried to calm her, gently taking Lottie's outstretched hands and leading her to one of the few benches in the town square which had survived unscathed, but her attempts to engage Lottie in conversation proved completely futile.

Maya's desperation meant that she couldn't stay for more than a couple of minutes, and she had to leave Lottie alone on the bench, staring blankly ahead, her long blonde hair lank and stained. As Maya walked away she stepped, almost unthinking, over the stream of water trickling from the cracked stone fountain that had once taken pride of place in the middle of the town.

Her tentative steps had quickly turned into a jog on unwilling, wobbling legs, then a sprint, arms pumping, heart hammering against her rib cage so hard it almost felt like it was pulling her forward with each heavy beat, dragging her home.

They had found her a few hours later, standing in the middle of what had once been her home. All that had been left of her old bedroom had been a dark, ruined stain on the ground, but she had still recognised it... felt it. There had been no sign of her mother or father, but in the one corner of their house which had miraculously escaped unharmed was a small stove, and on that was a pot of her mum's stew that she somehow always had ready whenever Maya returned home. Although the stew had been cold, the fragrant smell of the spices had still wafted across the wreckage and held her in place.

Maya had only realised that she was no longer alone when she had heard a gentle, slightly embarrassed cough. When she turned it was to see an odd pairing of characters. The first of the two was a tall, slim limbed and slightly round-stomached Sornette, with a face more suited to smiles than its current sorrowful gaze, the other a short and dour-looking Drömer who appeared to be far more comfortable with misery.

"What do I do now?" she'd asked them, not caring that they were strangers, all of her normal defensiveness and natural suspicion lost along with her home.

The tall Sornette had extended a long-fingered hand.

"I'm Lucid."

He'd taken her hand gently in his, his eyes brimming with sympathetic tears that Maya had been unable to find in herself.

"I can't tell you what to do, but I can give you another option. The Lady sent us to find you. She told us that we would find a new member of the Five here..." he'd paused and looked down for a moment in embarrassment, ashamed to intrude upon her grief. "But I am so sorry that it had to be under these circumstances."

It had all been too much to take in, her mind overwhelmed by the sudden loss of her home and family. Unable to really understand what she was being asked, and completely at a loss of what to do next, she had just nodded dumbly and let them lead her gently away, the quiet jangle of the Threads she had so carefully hoarded unheard and forgotten.

CHAPTER 5

Maya's foot caught the edge of a stray rock, making her stumble and returning her concentration fully to the present with an unpleasant crash, shredding the memories that the Horror had brought back and scattering them to the wind. As her eyesight cleared and she took in her surroundings she realised that, while her mind had been trapped in the past, her body had kept running without direction, blindly fleeing from the Horror, from the swarm of Nightmares, and from her own guilt at having left the strange glowing woman at the mercy of the monsters. But despite the overwhelming awfulness of the Horror and the menace of the Nightmares that had accompanied it, it was the memory of the tall blonde man and his empty smile that chilled her the most, spurring her to run even faster, sprinting until she felt her heart would burst.

In the distance she could still hear the roars of pursuit and she suspected, now that they had her scent, they would not stop until they had caught her, chasing her down until she was exhausted and could run no longer.

Maya narrowed her eyes and gritted her teeth with renewed determination. "Not in this lifetime," she muttered to herself. Now she was free of the influence of the Horror she was starting to think properly again, leaving behind the animal instinct to just run, instead she began planning out her next move like she had been trained to do. Changing direction, she pelted flat out through a more thickly wooded area, heading for what she hoped she remembered correctly as being a small shack alongside the Weave. A couple of minutes later and she was there, running straight past the shack and towards her actual goal, a small, flat bottomed dingy she had seen tethered, bobbing gently by the riverbank.

Cursing the boat's owner for their thoroughness, Maya tore at the knots securing the dingy in place, wincing at the sound of every cracking branch in the distance, each one closer and louder than the last. As the tether finally came loose the first of the chasing Nightmares burst through the treeline and dashed towards her, the speed of its approach aided by eight long, spindly legs.

"Great, more spiders," Maya groaned to herself as she threw the line clear, "why in the Dreamer's name does it always have to be spiders."

Keeping her eyes on the approaching Nightmare, which had slowed slightly (which was good) and was now snapping at her with several sets of huge, venomous and pointy teeth (which was definitely bad), Maya put one foot against the edge of the small boat and pushed back hard behind her, shoving it clear into the slow, drifting current of the Weave.

By now the spider creature was nearly on her, and several other Nightmares had now joined it, emerging one after another from among the trees. Maya tensed herself, shifting her weight onto the balls of her feet as the spider made the last few scuttling steps towards her. At the very last moment, just as it leapt for her, the front four legs flailing, she turned and jumped as hard and as far as she was able into the Weave, towards the dingy... or more precisely, towards the spot where she very much hoped the dingy still was.

To her incredible relief the boat hadn't yet drifted too far, and her leap took her just far enough to clutch hold of its edge before the whirling mists of the Weave swallowed her up. The pursuing spider wasn't quite so lucky, giving a brief snarl before turning to a dark, acrid smoke and scattering in the breeze as it made contact with the river of dreams.

There was nothing under her feet to get any purchase on, so Maya had to rely on the aching muscles in her arms to pull herself up. For one gut-wrenching moment it felt like she was going to pull the boat over, tipping herself back into the bottomless depths of the Weave. Then she was up, rolling flat onto her back, feeling the reassuring solidity of the dingy beneath her, her heart hammering against her chest and her breathing as heavy and unsteady as an elephant on a unicycle.

The Nightmares were massing on the bank closest to her, but none appeared willing to make the jump towards the dingy and risk the same fate as their spider comrade. It didn't stop them from making any number of aggressive growls, snarls and cries, which Maya presumed were either threats or insults... or both. Then the cries stopped, and the Nightmares all turned away from Maya and stared back towards the trees. There was a rustle of leaves and the broad-shouldered figure of the strange blonde man exited the undergrowth.

Even at this distance Maya could see his smile broaden as he spotter her, reaching out in her direction with one outstretched hand, as if he could pluck her from the boat as easily as picking a flower or lifting a child's doll from a shelf. Although the small part of her brain which was determinedly doing its best to stay rational (despite the increasingly odd events of the last hour), insisting that he couldn't possibly reach or hurt her from this far away, she still increased the rate of her paddling and hunched as low as she could into the scant protection offered by the dingy.

As it turned out her gut reactions proved to be far better informed than the more rational part of her brain. There was a sudden and terrifying roar as a Nightmare that appeared to have emerged directly out of the man's open hand flew overhead, missing Maya by a matter of inches. The creature's initial roar turned into a disappointed snarl when it realised it had overshot its target, which then rapidly degenerated into a despairing wail and finally silence as it hit the surface of the Weave and vanished, leaving nothing but a rather nasty smelling wisp of smoke.

Risking a look back, even as she increased the rate of her paddling, Maya saw the man look quizzically at his hand as if he was appraising a piece of faulty equipment, his smile slipping for a moment before he stretched out his hand again, another patch of shadow beginning to form in the centre of his palm.

Not wanting to give him another chance to attack, Maya paddled even more frantically and hit the faster moving currents in the centre of Weave, the sudden change of speed nearly causing her to lose her footing. Then the flow took her around the nearest bend, away from the blonde stranger and his collection of Nightmare companions.

Maya slumped back, the adrenaline that had kept her moving completely drained, and long-delayed exhaustion finally caught up with her. As she lay on her back, letting the Weave carry her away, her vision began to swim, blurring in from the edges until it faded to nothingness and the comfort of sleep took her into its embrace.

CHAPTER 6

"Is she okay?"

"I don't know, she doesn't look good. Give her a prod."

"You do it, she looks grubby. I don't want to catch anything."

Groaning with effort, Maya managed to force one of her eyes open and took in as much of her surroundings as she was able. Her vision was misted with the after-effects of her prolonged sleep, so initially all she could see was a couple of small, vague outlines, one of which looked like it was about to poke her with an outstretched finger.

Even half-asleep her reactions were sufficiently tightly wound for her arm to snap out and brush the approaching hand aside.

"Ow!"

Maya blinked her other eye open and slowly things settled into focus. Just above her were the concerned, confused and slightly scared looking faces of two Sornette youngsters. The first of the two, standing slightly further away was a boy, who looked no older than ten, staring suspiciously at her like she was some sort of mysterious, newly discovered and possibly dangerous creature, rather than a person. The second was a young girl of a similar age, her slightly scruffy bowler hat sparsely decorated with a couple of strands of brightly coloured ribbon rather than the more complex decorations of an older Sornette. She was also clutching her hand and staring accusingly at Maya.

"You hurt me!"

Pushing herself up onto her elbows Maya looked around, still confused as to where she was, how she had got to... wherever she was, and why a couple of Sornette children were now prodding her.

"Sorry?" she managed, rather half-heartedly.

She was still lying in the small dingy, but she could no longer feel the gentle rocking of the Weave beneath her. It seemed that she had washed up somewhere, beached on a shallow bank, nestled amongst clusters of the reeds that lined the river's edge. Behind the youngsters Maya could see the distant outline of Sornette barges, the gathering dusk illuminated by the glow of their campfires, trails of smoke winding lazily into the sky.

"Where am I exactly?" Maya asked, wondering how far she had drifted while she slept, and more importantly what had happened to her pursuers. Slowly she rose to her feet, wobbling slightly on weary legs.

"What's it to you," the boy shot back, still distrustful, glaring at Maya over the younger girl's shoulder.

"Could you show me back to your camp... please?" Maya asked, "I really need to get back to Nocturne, so if one of your traders is heading that way then perhaps...?"

She left the question hanging, hoping that one of them would complete it for her, but instead of giving her an answer the two Sornette youngsters leant in towards each other to hold a quick whispered conversation that Maya couldn't quite make out.

"Whisper, whisper, mutter, mutter... not sure about her."

"Whisper, whisper, grumble, mutter... maybe we could ask, mutter, mutter."

"Hhmpff... whisper, whisper," the girl concluded, seeming to have come to a decision, which the Sornette boy seemed less than happy with.

"You can come with us to see the Maman," the girl told Maya, while the boy continued to glower at her silently, managing an impressively disapproving look for one so young. "She can decide what's best to do with you."

"Fine," Maya replied, well aware that her best chance of getting to Nocturne quickly was to hitch a ride on a Sornette barge, and that the quickest way to do that would be to get the blessing of the local Maman, "lead the way."

The gathering was a pretty small one, no more than a dozen of the long, shallow-bottomed barges clustered alongside the banks of the Weave. The vessel that the two youngsters led Maya towards was right in the centre of the gathering and was slightly larger and more gaudily decorated than its neighbours. Maya thought she recognised the pattern of interlocking crescent moons that was repeated across the flags and canvas sheets that adorned the barge's deck, the symbol of one of the more minor clans that she had come across a few times in the docks when she had been running jobs for Granny. There was something else about the clan symbol that was familiar, tickling away at the back of her brain, but she couldn't quite place it. She was however certain that she hadn't met with the clan's leader, its Maman, in any of those previous encounters, so she wasn't exactly sure how she was going to be received now.

It was clear that news of her arrival had preceded her. The deck of the Maman's barge was pretty crowded, with most of the transient Sornette population from the surrounding vessels gathered together to get a look at Maya.

The two youngsters were making the most of the moment, taking their time as they strolled majestically across the deck, nodding and waving extravagantly to the gathering like a tiny king and queen holding court. Despite their obvious enjoyment of this brief moment of fame, the two young Sornette stopped their showboating as they drew close to the table set at the far end of the barge. The girl pulled gently on Maya's sleeve, encouraging her to pause for a moment and pointed to the bundle of robes heaped behind the desk.

"That's the Maman," she told Maya, "if anyone is going to help you it will be her."

"Thanks," Maya replied, giving the girl a brief smile to show her gratitude. It wasn't an expression that Maya's face was used to making, and from the look of alarm that flashed across the little Sornette's face, Maya was pretty sure it had come out as a grimace or snarl.

"Wow," she heard the boy mutter to himself, "that is a scary face."

Her brief attempt to re-arrange her expression into something less threatening didn't really seem to help much, so giving it up as a bad job, Maya settled for giving the two kids a final wave as she approached the heavy wooden table.

Although she hadn't met this particular Maman, she had dealt with several others and was aware of the appropriate etiquette. She stood patiently until a hand emerged from the bundled robes and gestured to the seat nearest to where Maya was standing. Another hand poking out from the other side of the robes reached up and pulled back what turned out to be a hood, revealing the oldest face that Maya had ever seen, nestled below a wide-brimmed hat that was flexing back into shape now it was no longer covered. The brim slowly spread out, its edges uncurling like the wings of a particularly ugly butterfly newly released from its cocoon.

As with all Sornette, the hat was ornately decorated, and from the number of decorative knick-knacks which were knotted, pinned and generally festooned all around it, this Maman was possibly the most ancient Sornette Maya had ever seen. There was enough brick-a-brack, haberdashery, flimflammery and shiny, worthless tat to fill several small market stalls. At the back of her mind Maya was secretly impressed with the strength the old Sornette must have in her neck muscles just to support the weight of the hat and its associated adornments.

"Thank you for agreeing to see me," she began, "I am grateful... and also to the young ones from your clan who found me."

The wizened face creased into something that might have been a smile, or perhaps a frown, or pretty much any expression, its true meaning disguised by the number of wrinkles and creases in the old woman's skin, every change in expression spreading outwards from her mouth like ripples in a pond.

"Heh, they were as excited as jitters to find you," the old woman began. Her voice gentle and melodious, far younger sounding than Maya was expecting. "They thought you must be a great warrior or adventurer... or something equally exciting."

Although she hadn't asked the question outright, Maya could sense the unspoken, but obvious query in the Maman's softly spoken words. In the most polite way possible she knew what she was really being asked was, "who or what are you, why are you here and are you a danger?"

"I'm no warrior," Maya began, which was true enough. She had fought, plenty of times, but it had always been back alleys and stealth, sneakiness and unwelcome necessity, none of which she felt qualified her as anything better than a thug for hire.

Despite her generally comfortable relationship with deception and half-truths she could feel the keen gaze of the Maman burning into her and knew that she would have to be honest. She had dealt with enough of the Sornette to realise that there would be no chance of bamboozling the wizened old woman sat opposite her. The soft exterior, the bundles of shapeless clothes, the huge soft brimmed hat sagging under the weight of a lifetime's collected knick-knacks, all of it was a special type of camouflage.

Underneath all that harmless-looking softness and the gentle questions was a mind sharpened by countless years spent leading a Sornette Clan through the daily complexities of trade and barter, of solving every type of personal and professional dispute. Maya also knew that if the Maman genuinely felt she was a risk to the clan, the open friendliness of the Sornette would fade like the mist of Weave itself, and if that happened then she would be lucky to make it off the barge.

"I didn't mean to end up here," Maya continued, taking a bit of a gamble and hoping that the thought that had just occurred to her was correct. "I just wanted to get back to Nocturne... to the Five."

"The Five?" the Maman repeated, half to herself. "Now that's a name I haven't heard in a while. One of mine joined the Five once upon a time, many years ago now. Good people... on the whole, but always in the middle of trouble of some kind or another." She paused her ponderings and leant forward, resting the bottom-most of her chins onto the arch of her hands. Sharp blue eyes, undimmed by the age that mottled the surrounding skin, stared up at Maya. "So, what kind of trouble are you in young lady?"

Maya inwardly congratulated herself, her memory hadn't let her down. The symbol of the interlocking moons was one she had seen many times but paid little attention to, every time she had walked down the portrait corridor back at the Five's Mansion in Nocturne. One of the more recent paintings, although still a couple of generations before the one including Maya, had shown a tall, thin-faced and unsmiling Sornette who had worn a clasp with that exact design.

Thinking back to the portrait corridor triggered another memory, and for a passing moment Maya felt like she was on the cusp of solving the mystery of the glowing woman who had sent her down this path.

However, she could still feel the Maman's gaze upon her, its intensity undiminished despite this minor breakthrough and Maya knew she needed to avoid any distractions and gather her thoughts, realising that this would be the moment where she would commit herself. Either the Maman would agree to help her and send her on her way, or...

Making a determined, conscious decision not to think about the alternatives, Maya looked directly into the eyes of the ancient Sornette.

"There is a Horror heading this way, a bad one," she began.

If she had expected a reaction to this news, she didn't get one, the Maman just continuing to stare, leaving a silent void for Maya to fill.

"I was sent to report on it, but there is something different about this one. It's not random like the others I have seen, it seems... it seems to know where it's heading."

Now she had started her explanation it was easier to keep going, the words tumbling out her mouth, unplanned and uncensored, the relief at being able to share her worries with someone overriding her natural caution.

"And it was accompanied by Nightmares. It was like they were guarding it, making sure that it gets to wherever it's heading. I don't know how far away it is, I don't even know how long I was asleep before your people found me, but I do know that I have to get to Nocturne as quickly as possible. I have to let the rest of the Five know and... and I really need your help to do that... please."

As she wound down, hoping desperately that she hadn't gone too far, she could see the cogs turning in the Maman's head. The old woman closed her eyes for a minute, sinking her chin even lower onto her hands as she thought. Then, seeming to have come to a conclusion, her eyes snapped back open and she barked out a command.

"Distra, tell the others to prepare the barges in case we need to depart in a hurry and send out a couple of scouts. If a Horror is headed this way, I want to know how long we have."

A tall figure that Maya had failed to spot, despite her well-trained powers of observation, detached itself from the shadows behind the table and gave a shallow bow in the Maman's direction before striding off across the barge. Unlike the other Sornette, this one was dressed in a sombre black suit, the hat completely unadorned, without any sort of trinket or other record of their life. Maya inwardly gave a sigh of relief, fairly sure that if the conversation had gone a different way the shadowy figure would have been instructed to deal with her instead.

"An odd group, the Five," the Maman said, pushing herself up from her seat, "but a useful one. Some say that there's no longer any need for people like you, that the true monsters of the past are long gone and forgotten... but I disagree. I will send you to Nocturne with one of my barges, make sure I don't regret that decision."

Ignoring Maya's awkward thanks, the Maman turned away and shuffled off across the deck, joined by several more Sornette and immediately entered into a series of muttered conversations, sending one after another of them running from the barge, presumably preparing the clan for departure as soon as possible.

Across at the other end of the deck, a Sornette trader beckoned her over. Maya presumed, from the look of his top hat (which was only partially decorated and rather shabby), that he was a relative youngster at the start of his trading career.

"I'm Barrow," he said with a cheerful grin as she reached him. "The Maman asked me to be your guide back to Nocturne, which should work out quite nicely as I have a cargo of spices that I need to offload pretty quickly, and Nocturne is as good a place as any."

He gestured across to a spot where Maya could see a small and rather rickety-looking barge moored slightly away from the main cluster of vessels.

"That's my girl over there. Best, fastest and most beautiful boat in all of Reverie. We'll get you to Nocturne before you know it."

As she drew closer Maya had a number of quite serious questions about the little barge, not least that it appeared to be cobbled together from bits of other boats, packing crates and what looked worryingly like a children's playhouse as the small cabin area. Someone had also enthusiastically, but with a complete lack of artistic talent, scrawled the name 'Belinda' close to the boat's bow.

"Very... nice?" Maya managed.

"Thanks, I built her myself, although you would never know it," Barrow told her proudly, without a touch of irony in his voice.

"Impressive," was about as far as Maya felt she could commit herself, without making her true feelings too obvious.

As Maya stepped lightly from the bank onto the deck of the barge, she thought that she could feel the planks flex under her feet, which was not the most promising start to their journey. This initial worry was immediately made worse as Barrow jumped past her and bounded enthusiastically to the rear of the deck, apparently completely unaware that every step caused the whole boat to shake unsteadily. Returning to the centre of the barge with one of the long poles the Sornette used to punt their vessels along the sides of the Weave, he gave Maya a quick wink and pushed off.

CHAPTER 7

To Maya's secret surprise and rather more obvious relief, the ramshackle vessel didn't immediately sink and after a couple of minutes they were underway, Barrow switching to a small sail once they were clear of the other barges and had entered a wider section of the Weave. Risking sitting down on the flat cushions that Barrow had dragged out from the small cabin, Maya allowed herself a brief moment of peace, closing her eyes and trying to use one of the mental tricks she had picked up during her time working the docks. With each inward breath she took in the peace and tranquillity of the surrounding Weave, and with each slow exhalation she visualised the panic and trauma of the Horror leaving her body and gently drifting away.

She had nearly reached a point where she was able to feel a modicum of calm when her relaxation was interrupted by Barrow's chirpy voice. "So, now we are on our way and away from the Maman, why don't you tell me what really happened to you? Run into some trouble with the locals, deal gone bad, crossed the wrong people?"

Maya's eyes snapped open indignantly. While what Barrow was suggesting was perhaps true of her previous time in Nocturne, where she had crossed paths with plenty of unpleasant characters and had made more than her fair share of enemies, (and some even worse friends), since she had joined the Five she had kept herself pretty consistently on the right side of the law. Her role as the Five's main scout and information gatherer had brought with it the additional benefit of keeping her well away from Nocturne for long periods of time, leaving those unsavoury connections far behind her.

"As it happens, everything that I told the Maman was completely true," she said, trying to push herself back up off the cushions where she had been reclining with as much aggrieved dignity as she could muster. "There was a Horror, one that was far worse than normal, and there were Nightmares with it... a lot of them. I was lucky to get away, I doubt that I would have if it hadn't been for..."

She paused, thinking back to the clash between the strange glowing woman and the tall blonde man leading the Nightmares. For the first time she had the chance to think about the encounter without some immediate danger to distract her, and she was increasingly sure that the woman had been a Daydreamer.

Maya had never met one herself, but occasionally Lucid or Grimble would talk about past members of the Five, and although they had spoken of her rarely and even then, only in hushed tones, the snippets of tales they had shared were about a young woman from the Waking World with incredible powers.

Still, Maya couldn't recall seeing a portrait which included the woman in the Mansion's corridor and wondered what must have taken place for such an extraordinary being to be written out of the history of the Five.

"If it hadn't been for what?" Barrow asked, leaning casually on the rail of the barge, half an eye on Maya and half on the route ahead of them.

"Nothing... I was just lucky to get away from them, and now I need to get to Nocturne."

The jaunty angle of Barrow's eyebrow made it very clear that he didn't believe her, but he didn't push her on the subject, just nodded in the direction of the Weave stretching out in front of them.

"Don't worry, like I said Belinda is the fastest barge in all of Reverie. We will get you there."

He paused, apparently turning over a thought in his mind that he found particularly pleasing. "And then when you save the world or whatever, you can tell them it was thanks to the help of me and my girl here." He patted the rail affectionately, eyes sparkling with the enthusiasm of the newly heroic.

Maya pretended not to notice the fact that the shaky rail had left a large splinter in Barrow's palm as he continued.

"And then I will be able to charge a small fortune for the privilege of travelling on the boat that saved the day."

They had been travelling for nearly a full day when Maya realised that something was wrong. Barrow had left her to her own devices for a while, getting bored when she refused to share any of the more grisly tales from her time spent in Nocturne with him. He wasn't sulking exactly, but definitely had the look of someone who had expected something rather more exciting from his mysterious passenger than stories about bartending, working long hours and learning to live with a leaky roof.

Maya had been staring towards the horizon, desperate for the first sight of the spires of Nocturne to drift into view, but so far she had been disappointed, and suspected she would be for some time yet, despite Barrow's insistence that they were currently breaking all known records for speed of travel down the Weave. She had quickly grown to doubt his ever-confident claims, particularly when earlier in their journey a donkey had ambled slowly past on the nearby bank, gradually overtaking them before finally disappearing into the distance with a dismissive swish of its tail. Admittedly they had picked up their pace since then, Barrow blaming a sudden drop in the wind that had left the small sail flat and lifeless for nearly an hour, but it hadn't helped with Maya's growing anxiety.

Because her attention had been fixed on what was ahead, initially she had failed to see the dark ripple that had flowed across the surface of the Weave behind them, a small, insistent oil-slick sat unpleasantly on top of the gently flowing mists, slowly closing in on their vessel. The first she knew of it was when Barrow called out to her in a voice which, while not completely panicked, was certainly several steps away from his normal cheery confidence, as well as being at least a strained octave higher.

"What in the Great Dream is that?" he asked her, pointing at their odd pursuer.

Maya squinted, trying to make out the small patch of shadow in more detail. It wasn't like anything she had seen before, but despite this, some inner animal part of her knew without doubt that whatever that thing was, it was something bad.

"I don't know. But I don't think it would be a good idea to let it catch up with us... whatever it is."

Barrow gulped and nodded, "I think I agree with you."

By now the murky stain was less than fifty metres away, and if anything Maya got the feeling it was moving slightly faster, closing in on them now it had sight of its prey.

"Isn't there anything you can do? Whatever that thing is, it's nearly on us!"

Barrow lifted his top hat and scratched his head. "Uhm. There is something, but it's a bit experimental. You know I said that Belinda was the fastest vessel on the Weave?"

Maya nodded, "I remember you saying that... a lot, but I haven't seen much evidence of it."

"Well, she is, or was... or could be... I made a few modifications that worked really well, for a while... and then... um... boom."

Maya could see the dark shadow even more clearly now it was so close behind them, and although she couldn't explain why, the prospect of the barge going 'boom' was still preferable to being caught by whatever it was pursuing them. Even though it was entirely flat, clinging to the surface of the Weave like a second skin, the shadowy, shapeless form nevertheless gave Maya the impression of incredible depth, of teeth and claws and awfulness.

"I'll risk it," she told Barrow. "Whatever it is you need to do, do it now."

Shrugging in a way that obviously meant, "don't say I didn't warn you," Barrow reached down and pulled a lever that Maya had ignored up until now, presuming that it was just another of the random decorations that adorned the barge. There was a creaking, painful sounding rumble that shook the whole of the deck and an odd-looking contraption juddered upright, emerging from under a pile of sacking right at the back of the vessel. It looked like a tiny windmill, three wooden arms folding out from a central hub, all balanced at the top of a slim metal column, no taller than Maya.

"Hold on to your hat," Barrow shouted, following his own advice and gripping the brim of his top hat tightly with his left hand. With his other hand he reached down and pulled at a cord hanging loosely from the base of the strange device, which sputtered into immediate life. The blades of the windmill began to spin, initially sluggishly, but increasingly quickly, and as they did Maya could feel the barge begin to increase in speed as the artificially generated wind caught in the small sail, stretching it taut.

"It's working," Maya shouted across to Barrow, the miniature turbine creating a surprising amount of noise, threatening to snatch her words away before they reached him. Behind them the shadowy shape was no longer gaining, instead it was now slowly dropping back. If it was possible for an empty, apparently lifeless patch of shadow to give off a sense of frustration or anger, then this one definitely did. Maya was pretty sure that the surface of the pursuing darkness rippled slightly, bubbling and pulsing as it too increased in speed, skimming across the Weave. Even with this extra spurt of effort, the Barge was managing to slowly draw away as the speed of the rotors continued to increase, although this was all at some cost to the surrounding vessel.

The column supporting the turbine was shuddering violently, the hinged bracket holding it in place threatening to rip itself clear of the deck at any moment. The small sail was also very obviously being over-stretched by the amount of pressure the increased wind was putting on it, almost dragging the small barge across the surface, the edges beginning to fray and pull away from the mast.

"How long will it last?" Maya pointed to the erratically spinning rotors, trying to make herself heard above the wind and the increasingly loud rattling sounds coming from the rest of the boat.

"I don't know," Barrow shouted back. "Last time it didn't even last this long."

"What happened last time," Maya began, then stopped herself. "Actually, don't tell me, I presume it went 'Boom.'"

"Boom," Barrow confirmed with an entirely inappropriate grin, accompanied by a hand gesture that effectively mimed a scene in which the little barge exploded into tiny pieces. For someone on a rickety barge, which was almost certainly shaking itself to pieces, he seemed remarkably cheery.

Maya tried to comfort herself with the thought that, should that happen, it would be the least of their problems. If they survived the destruction of the barge then they would end up falling, potentially forever, into the depths of the Weave. A Weave that they would be sharing with a malevolent shadow... thing. Maya cursed quietly to herself, her train of thought turning out to be the exact opposite of comforting.

Realising, rather bitterly, that there was nothing she could do, other than cling grimly onto the barge's shaking rail and hope that the Dreamer would watch over them, she closed her eyes and hoped for the best, or at least that they could avoid the worst. After what seemed like an eternity, during which time the insistent background rattling had increased to a pained, screeching whine that promised imminent destruction, Maya was disturbed by a tap on her shoulder.

"I think we might be alright." Barrow was grinning proudly. "That strange shadowy thing has gone, or at least it's so far behind that I can't see it anymore... and even better than that, look..." he pointed into the distance.

There, on the horizon was the wonderfully familiar sight of the tallest spires of Nocturne, rising above the mist of the Weave and calling her home, like the beckoning fingers of a long-lost friend that she feared she would never see again. Deciding that discretion, and possibly survival, was the better part of valour, Barrow agreed to turn off the miniature turbine. He couldn't completely hide his disappointment that he wouldn't be entering the bustling dockyards of Nocturne at breakneck speed, pursued by shadowy monsters, which he obviously felt would do his credibility a great deal of good. However, his decision was pretty much made for him when a fairly important-looking piece of the contraption came flying off and whizzed past his face. The small, red hot shard of metal only stopped when it hit the barge's mast, embedding itself deeply into the wood and sizzling gently.

As they drew closer, at a slightly more sedate pace than the rest of their journey, the sight of the approaching docks, grimy and unpleasant as they were, was like a breath of fresh air to Maya. In direct contrast to the more elegant towers in the centre of the city, the docks were squat and low, gathered around the base of the newer and more attractive parts of Nocturne.

Maya, perhaps because of her farming background, or more likely just because she was very perceptive and had immediately recognised the docks for what they were, had always thought of the docks as being the equivalent of the manure surrounding and feeding taller and more elegant crops. Grubby and squalid, often overlooked, always smelly, but completely essential to the life of the rest of the city. Standing at the very front of the small vessel she took a deep breath, then gagged slightly. Perhaps not like a breath of fresh air after all, she corrected herself, but a breath of familiar air at least.

When she recovered enough for her eyes to stop watering, she drummed her fingers impatiently on the edge of the barge's rail. Although it was only a few minutes away she could hardly stand the delay. She needed to feel the ground under her feet and get herself to the Mansion. With Barrow's rather unique and dangerous approach to helping, she had managed to outrun whatever it was that had been chasing her, but the main threat was still out there. Somewhere to the West a Horror like nothing she had ever seen was coming and she needed to warn the Five.

After that she wasn't really sure what would happen, nor did she particularly care. It had never been her job. Her role was to scout, which is what she always did. Then she would share whatever she had managed to find with the rest of the Five, and they would sort out whatever needed sorting out. It was a transactional relationship that she was entirely happy with. She would hand across information and the subsequent complications of decision making, moral choices, balancing risks and benefits, and everything else that followed, would be dealt with by the other members of the group, all of whom Maya felt were far better qualified than she was.

As the barge bumped gently into the wood of the nearest jetty, Maya shouted a brief thanks back across her shoulder to Barrow, who was looking a little deflated, his entry to the city having been far less exciting and flamboyant than he had obviously wished. If she had more time she would have pointed out that still being alive was probably more than they could have hoped for earlier in the day, but in the circumstances the best she could do was give him a final wave as she leapt nimbly off the vessel and raced off across the docks.

All sorts of sailors and traders, plus a handful of reputable looking merchants and a much larger number of shadier characters all whipped past in a blur, either dodged around or barged aside without a second thought.

The grubbier surroundings of the docks gradually gave way to the cleaner streets of the city, the uneven wooden planks flexing under Maya's feet as she sprinted becoming evenly spaced paving slabs. Finally, the welcome sight of the Mansion appeared in the distance, standing out amongst the more ordered surrounding buildings. The sight was so welcome that she almost failed to spot the shadow that flickered across the window of the nearest house, but even after everything she had been through, the ever-aware part of Maya that had served her so well in the past screamed a warning.

She didn't know how it had caught up with her, but she was certain that it was the same shadowy being that had pursued them on the surface of the Weave. Waves of misery, similar to those Maya had felt as she passed the Horror, washed over her, but this time she fought off the feelings of despair and instead she dug deep into her dwindling reserves of energy.

Sprinting even faster, Maya covered the last few metres of her run to the Mansion in a matter of seconds, jinking through the gardens and avoiding the plants and twisting weeds that tried to impede her progress as they snapped at her ankles. As she cleared the garden and reached the main building, she could feel the chill of the shadow just behind her, so it was an incredible relief to see the heavy door swing open, the gently glimmering form of the Lady filling the doorway.

"Shadow... behind me... a Horror, a Horror is coming..." Maya gasped between painful breaths as she slowed, the safety of the Mansion almost within her reach. She knew that the shadowy form could only be a matter of metres behind her, but she was confident that the Lady would be more than a match for whatever the thing pursuing her could be, having proved herself time and again to be indomitable when facing all manner of challenges.

So it made absolutely no sense to Maya as she watched the glowing shape of the Lady slowly step back into the Hallway and the heavy front door begin to close.

"What... what are you doing?" She cried, her initial confusion giving way to fear as she felt the chill of the shadow reaching her. "Help me..."

Through the remaining slim gap between the dark wood of the Mansion's door and the surrounding frame she could just about make out the ice blue slivers of the Lady's eyes, staring back at her, filled with something close to remorse.

A gentle whisper, "I'm sorry," drifted into Maya's ears, almost too soft to hear, and then the door clicked shut with a finality that echoed in her mind.

Weighed down by exhaustion and an increasing coldness that she could no longer ignore or fight, Maya's limbs gave way under her, and she sank into a heap, her head resting against the front door of the Mansion. She knew that the shadow must be on her by now, and the temptation to just give in was overwhelming, but the stubborn core that she had inherited from her parents, and which she had refined over the years, firstly down in the docks and then scouting for the Five, wouldn't allow it.

With a superhuman effort she slowly turned her head, determined to face her pursuer face-on one last time. As she did so, she was confronted by the sight of the black, shadowy form stretching out across the closest slabs of the Mansion's hotchpotch footpath, spinning slowly. The sight was oddly hypnotic, and she found that now she had seen it she couldn't look away. Rather than being afraid, she found it oddly calming, the need to fight, to resist ebbing away. Then as she stared more and more deeply into the whirling darkness, losing the last of her sense of place and time, there was a discordant shrieking sound and the blackness sprang up to meet her.

CHAPTER 8

Maya awoke with a bump, her recent memories of the flight to the Mansion, the Lady's unfathomable betrayal and her fall into the shadow all fighting for space in her head. Every part of her ached, even her teeth, and when she tried to push herself off the ground all she achieved was a horrible sense of vertigo, before collapsing flat onto her back again. Her predicament wasn't improved when a large and unpleasant face loomed over her.

"Got another one," it rasped to some unseen companion. "Looks like this one is freshly arrived."

Maya blinked, her brain unsuccessfully trying to catch up with the rapid rate at which things around her kept changing. The face above her was unmistakably that of a Nightmare, it had far too many eyes, teeth and apparent dental hygiene issues to be anything else. She grimaced, turning her head away slightly. Until she had been sent to check on the most recent Horror, she had never seen a Nightmare other than one chasing its assigned dreamer, in the shape of whatever creature, monster or other inexplicable object of fear took their dreamer's fancy.

They had never paid her or anyone else any attention at all, just focusing on the job in hand, which was always to chase and not quite catch their Dreamer. Now it seemed she couldn't go more than a few steps without some sort of Nightmare creature being on her case, and the rules about not catching people definitely didn't seem to apply.

"What..." she began, but her question was cut off by a pointed snarl from the creature looming above her.

"Silence," it growled. "You are in the realm of Ephialtes, Queen of the Nightmares. You will not speak, you will not question, but you will work."

Now her head had cleared a little, Maya tried to push herself upright again, this time with more success and was able to get a better look at her surroundings. The first thing she noticed was that she was seated in a large cavern, dark rock stretching off into the distance in all directions. The second was that her ankles and wrists were shackled together with heavy metal chains, the third was that the scary visage of the Nightmare was attached to a rather less terrifying body.

The creature she was faced with was no more than three feet tall, with scrawny looking arms and short, slightly bowed legs attached to a round, furry middle. The creature's head made up nearly half its total size, and while it was still scowling at her in a menacing manner, now she could see it more clearly Maya wondered if the grimace was quite as scary as she had first thought, looking more like a short-sighted squint than a glare.

"I am Kreepa, Overlord of the dungeons of Ephialtes, Supreme commander of the Mines of Scaar, Master of the...." it continued, gesticulating grandly, apparently unaware its new captive was less than overwhelmed with terror, but Maya didn't get to hear what it was master of, as the speech was interrupted by a shout from across the cavern.

"Kreepa, you little Grunlit, hurry up and bring the new prisoner. We've got a quota to keep to."

The little Nightmare growled something under its breath and then clapped its hands together sharply a couple of times. In response to its summons Maya heard a series of heavy footsteps from behind her, and another Nightmare stomped past her, reached down and picked up Kreepa in one huge hand. It was pretty much the exact opposite of its companion, with a huge, muscular body topped with a particularly tiny head. The whole thing was finished off with a small tuft of bright red hair standing almost completely upright from the centre of its skull. It now stood cradling Kreepa protectively against its chest, balanced on the flat palm of one giant, gnarled hand, which brought the smaller Nightmare back up to Maya's eye line.

"This way prisoner," Kreepa grunted, although this time rather half-heartedly, and the larger Nightmare prodded Maya in the shoulder with its free hand, pushing her in the direction of an opening in the far wall of the cavern. "Welcome to the rest of your life..."

As Maya shuffled through, she was greeted with the sight of an even larger cavern than the one she had just left. The walls were made of the same dark, slightly melted looking rock, but everything else was completely different. The place was crowded with other prisoners, shackled like Maya. A mix of Sornette, Drőmer and other residents of Reverie. Some were hacking despondently at piles of rubble with a variety of worn-looking tools, while others were clustered around a slow-moving conveyor, picking through smaller chunks of rock. Right in the centre of the cavern, the whole place was dominated by a huge construction, a scaffold tower containing a massive stone pillar which was gradually being winched upwards, pulled by a series of chains dragged by yet more prisoners. There was a drumbeat from somewhere far across the cave and the pillar dropped, shaking the foundations of the whole place.

A tall, gangly and very unpleasant looking Nightmare ambled across to them, clicking its claws impatiently. "Bring her over, we need another one in Sorting."

Muttering under its breath, Kreepa pointed Maya in the direction of the nearest conveyor. "This will be your work area until you are told otherwise. One of the others will show you what to do."

"What about food?" Maya asked, scowling back and ignoring Kreepa's shocked inhalation, presumably because she had dared to speak.

"You eat at the end of the day. If you are very lucky and find one of the stones that we are mining for, then you get double rations." Kreepa smiled unpleasantly at this, making Maya immediately suspect that the promise of extra food might not be that much of a benefit. This was reinforced when one of the figures hunched over the nearby conveyor looked up for a moment, gave Maya a nervous grin, mimed being sick, then immediately looked down again, doing a very passable impression of someone studiously chipping away at the boulder in front of them.

"Pah, it's no good acting tough once you're here in the Mines," Kreepa gestured around the cavern, taking in the various clusters of despondent looking workers. "Once you're here you never leave. You will just work, every single day for the rest... of... your... life." The last few words were artificially stretched out, presumably to add some menace to what Kreepa was saying, but Maya ignored it, already looking around the cavern to try and identify any points of weakness or opportunity for escape.

"How about you, you here every day too?" she asked pointedly.

Kreepa just scowled, which pretty much confirmed what Maya was beginning to suspect.

"I think that you hate it here too, almost as much as the prisoners, don't you," she said, but although he flushed a dark purple and his scowl deepened even further, Kreepa didn't answer, just clicked his fingers. In response the massive Nightmare carrying him span on the spot and then marched away, back in the direction they had come from, leaving Maya alone with the group of workers gathered around the slowly moving piles of rocks. One of them nudged her gently and offered her a small hammer, then mimed hitting the nearest small rock, smiling encouragingly at Maya as they did so.

"Who are..." Maya began, but the man just put his finger to his lips and then pointed Maya back to the rocks.

"Fine, I get it... hit the rocks and don't speak," Maya said, her continuing speech seeming to cause the man actual physical pain. His eyes darted from side to side as he made a more desperate looking shushing motion.

She gave the nearest rock a desultory tap with the hammer, which received a firm thumbs up from her new companion, who looked incredibly relieved that she had decided to do what she was supposed to. As the day continued, she settled into a new, mind-numbing pattern of sorting and occasionally hitting a variety of stones, rocks and small boulders.

It was starting to feel like the shift would never end when there was a shrill whistle and the group Maya was standing with all dropped their tools. Then one by one, they all shuffled away from the conveyor that had been feeding Maya a steady supply of rocks for the last few hours.

As they walked slowly to the far side of the cave, they crossed paths with another group of prisoners, presumably taking their place, some of whom were still yawning and stretching.

"Where do we sleep?" Maya asked the woman she was standing next to, but this time being careful to keep her voice as quiet as possible.

The woman just shrugged in response, pointing at the nearest wall, then left Maya's side, walking across to the uneven edge of the cavern and slowly sitting down with a tired sigh.

Not really sure what else to do, Maya followed suit, although without the sigh. There didn't seem to be any sort of bedding or blankets, with most of the other workers wrapping their ragged clothes around them instead, although none of them seemed ready to lay down, despite their obvious exhaustion.

A couple of minutes later she realised why, as she was disturbed by the rattle of a giant metal trolley being pushed towards them. To her surprise, she recognised the characters pushing it. Or more specifically the hulking Nightmare with a tuft of red hair who was pushing it and the other much smaller figure of Kreepa riding on top, like a tiny and very grumpy jockey. Despite the desperate nature of her current predicament, Maya still felt a secret rush of delight when she saw that Kreepa was also wearing a little chef's hat and holding a ladle.

Pointedly ignoring Maya's incredulous stare, Kreepa started to spoon a gelatinous looking slop into shallow stone bowls, which his larger companion handed out to each of the collapsed workers. The nearest of them, who was very obviously starving after a day of hard labour, took a large spoonful. The expression on their face as they tried to swallow a mouthful for the first, second and even third time didn't fill Maya with any sort of confidence, the food valiantly resisting being eaten.

When it came to Maya's turn to eat, the bowl of shapeless goo was every bit as bad as she feared. She had no idea if it had once been some sort of meat, vegetable, fruit or anything else recognisable, but there was nothing else to eat, and at the least it seemed to have been enough to keep the other workers alive. After several failed attempts she managed to keep a few mouthfuls of the food down, pushing the parts of her brain respectively responsible for her taste buds and gag reflex right to the back of her mind, where they both muttered and grumbled rebelliously.

The night passed slowly, patches of fitful sleep interspersed with moments of unpleasant wakefulness, trying without success to find a less uncomfortable position before overwhelming tiredness dragged her back down into unconsciousness.

The following day was very much the same. A slow shuffle to the conveyor, interminable hours of tapping at an apparently endless carousel of rocks, none of which contained the mysterious gems that the Nightmares seemed so keen to find. Then another slow shuffle back to the wall and a bowl of the same unpalatable goop served up by the multi-talented Kreepa, who Maya was now pretty sure was more of a general dogsbody than Overlord.

The next day was the same again, and the next, and the next... each one blurring into the following, the permanent darkness of the cavern making the difference between day and night meaningless and soon forgotten. After a while she was even able to swallow the strange food without thinking too much about it.

Maya wasn't naturally given to despair, having dug herself out of any number of awkward, difficult or downright dangerous situations in her time. But this was different, the sheer drudgery and boredom was hard to shake off, weighing down on her more and more as time passed, until she found it hard to stand up straight. She had almost given up hope, feeling herself fading to grey like the other sorry souls trapped working in the Mines, when something happened, something big... and everything changed.

CHAPTER 9

It started out like any other day, which is to say, like any other day that Maya could remember, the memory of life outside of the Mines having faded like a picture left out in the sun. First the vibrant colour that filled her memories had withered away, then the outlines had also slowly dwindled, leaving nothing behind, just an empty frame around a blank canvas where the memory used to be.

She had been standing at her spot by the conveyor, eyes down, focusing on the pile of rock in front of her, having learned the hard way that looking around too much drew unnecessary and sometimes painful attention, when there was a huge reverberating bang that shook the entire cavern. The following shockwave was enough to knock Maya from her feet, her knees bumping painfully against the edge of the conveyor on her way down.

The scene that awaited her as she regained her feet and looked across the cavern was one of complete chaos. The huge scaffold in the centre of the cavern was veering unsteadily, the heavy stone pillar that had previously been sat securely within it was now hanging loosely to one side, the bottom section completely gone. As she watched the tortured metal of the huge construct gave one final, painful screech and then gave up its battle with gravity, dropping heavily to the ground. Amongst all the carnage she almost failed to spot the small group running desperately across the cave, somehow avoiding both the scattered debris and the Nightmare guards at the same time. There was a small, slightly built boy, sprinting with a look of total concentration on his face, a lanky Sornette, weaving easily between obstacles, and slightly behind them both, the compact figure of a heavily scarred and deeply miserable-looking Drőmer. The last figure, in particular, drew Maya's attention. In addition to the scowl on his face, even his running style managed to express extreme distaste for his surroundings, heavy feet stamping as he ran, as if he was taking out his frustrations on the cavern itself.

Even at this distance there was only one individual that Maya knew who could convey so much grumpiness so effectively.

"Grimble... Lucid, what in the Great Dream are you doing here?"

Off to one side, she also spotted a small group of prisoners who were shouting encouragement to the three runners. Maya had seen them before, but always at a distance and hadn't really paid them much attention. They were all clothed in bright, rather showy outfits and were also still remarkably cheerful-looking compared to most of the other workers in the cave. Right at the front was a tall, rather grand looking gentleman dressed as a ringmaster, top hat still perched on his head. Next to him was a small Drőmer dressed in an even more outlandish outfit, covered in sparkling stars. As Maya was watching, the Drőmer stuck out his foot to trip a Nightmare running past in the direction of the fleeing strangers.

Looking up he saw Maya staring is his direction and gave her a broad smile, sticking up one stubby thumb. It felt like a lifetime since Maya had seen anyone do anything except work, sleep or gulp down the disgusting goop they got fed every evening, but the sight of the smile was all it took for a spark of hope to re-ignite within her. Taking her cue from the little Drőmer, Maya shuffled in the direction of the nearest group of Nightmares as fast as her chains would let her, placing herself between them and the three would-be escapists.

As the group of Nightmares reached her, expecting to barge her out of the way, as they had any number of the other prisoners as they charged across the cavern, Maya dropped to the ground and managed to tangle the legs of at least three of them in the chains shackling her ankles and wrists. It hurt terribly, as the heavy weight of the Nightmares caught in the chains, yanking her arms so hard she felt like they were going to be pulled out of their sockets, but it was worth it. One after another they toppled over, crashing into their neighbours like monstrous skittles. For the first time in a long while Maya felt alive, unconcerned about her own wellbeing, but determined to do whatever she could to cause trouble for the Nightmares.

She was expecting some sort of immediate punishment, but the monsters seemed so keen on their pursuit that they ignored her completely, staggering back to their feet (or claws, or in one case flippers) before racing back off across the cave without a backward glance.

Rather gingerly Maya also regained her feet, trying not to put too much pressure on her aching shoulders as she pushed herself upright, then slowly made her way to the far wall, before sliding back down into a sitting position.

The odd group that had briefly caused all the fuss had disappeared into a tunnel at the far end of the cavern, hotly pursued by a huge mob of Nightmares, and the occasional cry of the chase could still be heard echoing back up from the tunnel and reverberating around the cavern.

With the giant pillar at the centre of the chamber out of commission, the whole mining operation had ground to a halt. Groups of workers stood in small, confused clusters, unsure as to what they were supposed to do now. The remaining Nightmares didn't seem to have any better ideas and settled for striding up and down making unpleasant faces at their prisoners or growling rather shallow threats. Eventually, even this low-grade bullying got boring, and the workers were all allowed to settle down against the far wall and rest, waiting to see what would happen next.

This turned out to be very little, the pause in the mining operation leaving the Nightmares as directionless and confused as their unfortunate prisoners. That evening Kreepa made his normal rounds, but even he seemed unusually distracted and could hardly manage even the most basic of insults as he ladled out the nightly portion of horrible food.

For the next few days nothing changed. The wreckage of the pillar and its surrounding scaffold a constant reminder of the unexpected explosion and the escape of the three strangers. The ache in Maya's limbs slowly faded away, the break from the constant cycle of work and fitful sleep giving her body the chance for some desperately needed rest. She had kept a watchful eye out for the other strange characters she had spotted across the cavern, the tall ringmaster and the unusually dressed Drőmer, but hadn't seen any sign of them since.

The Nightmares had begun the gradual process of bringing the mine back to a usable condition, several of them leading a despondent group of prisoners in the slow repair of the central scaffold. A second group were working on the reconstruction of a large wooden platform that had been crushed by the falling pillar.

The platform had previously been home to the mine's Overseer, a short menacing figure with huge glowing eyes that Maya had only ever seen from a distance. The few times when she had spotted the odd, distant shape perched on its eyrie, it had filled her with an indescribable cold sensation, and she had never been able to look long enough to see it very clearly. She had asked a few of the other prisoners about it, unsure as to exactly what the Overseer was, seeming to be neither a Nightmare or any of the other races of Reverie that she was familiar with, but her questions had been met with hurried shushes and frightened glances.

60

Since the escape there had been no sign of the Overseer, but on the fifth day, shortly after the repair work to the wooden platform was completed, it re-emerged and once again Maya could feel its malevolent gaze drifting across the cavern like a searchlight.

She had resigned herself to a slow, inexorable return to the previous depressing grind when another strange turn of events, even more cataclysmic than the last, shook the mine to its core. The first sign that something was amiss was when a shrill, shrieking cry went up from the Overseer's platform. Although there were no words that Maya could make out, the sense of anger was obvious and caused an almost instant reaction in the groups of Nightmares who had previously been aimlessly milling around in the cavern. Each of them lifted their heads, snouts or beaks and howled in reply, before rushing towards the exit. Somewhere in the distance Maya was sure she could hear the sounds of some sort of disturbance, with cries and shouts of battle rattling back down the nearest tunnels.

The squat figure of the Overseer dropped from its perch above the far exit, landing surprisingly lightly as it hit the ground, where it was joined by two of the largest and most unpleasant of the few remaining Nightmare guards. It made an impatient beckoning motion, pointing to where the small stash of the dark gems that the miners had collected were stored in a solid metal chest, which the two large Nightmares lifted between them.

Maya had a very strong feeling that whatever the Nightmares had in mind for the odd, black stones was not going to be good. She had heard a few whispered rumours about what they were used for, a couple of the longest-serving prisoners muttering darkly about the stones being some sort of energy source for the most powerful of the Nightmare creatures.

Looking at the two heavyset monsters slowly carrying the metal casket towards the exit, Maya thought back to the sense of release she had experienced when she had tangled the Nightmares in her chains during the previous escape, and decided in that split second that she was going to do whatever she could to obstruct, slow, or otherwise mess with whatever it was that the Nightmares were up to.

Her options were limited by the shackles that still restricted the movement of her arms and legs, so trying to cross the cavern in time to stop them wasn't really an option. What she quickly realised she did have was an almost limitless supply of small rocks, the discarded spoil of weeks of mining. Maya grabbed the nearest one, no bigger than a large pebble, and without stopping to think too much about the consequences, heaved it in the direction of the Overseer and its companions. Even after several weeks of hard labour and terrible food Maya's aim was pretty good, and the stone landed with a clunk on the thick skull of the nearest of the Nightmares carrying the metal chest.

The results were far better than she could have hoped for. The creature released its grip on the heavy chest to reach for the unexpected bump on its head, which turned out to be a big mistake as the far end of the metal container crashed to the ground, landing squarely on one of the Nightmares large, scaly feet. The resulting roar of pain startled its companion enough for it to also release its grip on the other end, and within moments the whole orderly arrangement was in tatters, the heavy metal chest on its side, contents spilling out across the cavern floor.

The Overseer swivelled its head to stare back across at the spot where Maya stood, her arm still raised from the throw. As the burn of its gaze washed across her, Maya quickly dropped her arm to her side but knew that this was unlikely to fool anyone. Her fear was immediately confirmed when the Overseer raised one arm (or possibly wing, Maya was still unsure exactly what she was looking at) and shrieked angrily in her direction.

The two hulking guards turned and advanced towards Maya, although one was quite badly slowed by a severely squashed looking foot, which it was dragging awkwardly behind the other. They were joined by a couple of other, smaller Nightmares that had remained within the Cavern, and the motley group marched grimly en-masse towards her.

Preparing for the worst, but making an inward pact with herself that whatever happened to her now it had been worth it, Maya scrabbled around for a couple more rocks and wound her arm back for another throw. Looking at the size of the approaching creatures it seemed unlikely she would achieve anything more than giving them a slightly awkward tickle, but at least she was going to go down fighting... or at least aggressively tickling.

When she threw the first of her stones she expected to see it bounce harmlessly off the closest of the approaching creatures, instead there was a loud 'crump' as a boulder, much larger than anything she would even be able to lift, let alone throw, flattened the nearest Nightmare. For the briefest of moments Maya wondered if the stones had some sort of previously ignored magical property that made them expand in mid-air, then the more practical part of her brain took control again and suggested she look back over her shoulder.

There, looking every bit as mad, bad and dangerous as any of the Nightmares, was a huge, hulking, but entirely familiar figure that she recognised immediately.

"Carter!" she exclaimed, forgetting herself and the grimness of their situation for a minute. She found it hard to believe her eyes, but Carter was pretty hard to mistake for anyone or anything else, other than perhaps a slightly slow, well-meaning but incredibly dangerous mountain... in a suit.

It had been several years since she had last seen him, when she had still been running errands for Granny down in the docks, where

Carter had been a constant figure in the background as Granny's loyal bodyguard, muscle and dogsbody.

"Ullo Miss," the massive figure replied, dropping his arm rather guiltily to one side. "Um... I didn't mean to hurt it that bad, it's just they looked pretty angry... and Granny always said to look out for you, cus you were one of hers."

"You still remember me then?"

"Course I do Miss," Carter replied, sounding rather hurt. Then he paused, looking past her, "Scuse me a moment."

He stepped past Maya, pushing her gently but firmly to one side and grabbed the two smaller Nightmares who had just stopped gawping at their squashed comrade and lifted them both into the air, one in each hand. Before they had a chance to do anything other than squawk angrily, he bashed the two of them together and then dropped them, leaving them lying stunned on top of the bigger Nightmare still trapped under the boulder.

The final Nightmare had just caught up with the rest, its injured foot having considerably slowed its progress. It wasn't normally that easy to tell what a creature with eight eyes and a set of teeth the size, shape, and colour of mossy rocks was thinking, but on this occasion Maya could tell it was suddenly extremely keen to be somewhere else.

Carter had picked up another massive boulder, which he was casually tossing up and down in one huge hand. This wasn't lost on the Nightmare, which had begun to shuffle backward, apparently having decided that discretion was the better part of valour. This was confirmed when it turned and began a slow, rather painful-looking half-run back towards the distant, furious figure of the Overseer.

"What's going on," Maya asked. "I thought that you couldn't hurt Nightmares... that they just turned to dust, or smoke or whatever and reappear again later."

"That's what normally happens," Carter said, "but I've been here a while now and I've worked a few things out." He gave Maya a shy smile, obviously quite proud of himself. "They do that everywhere else, and when they disappear... this is where they come back to."

"And?"

"And when they're here, where they all come from, seems to me like fings are a bit different. If they get squashed here..." he pointed to the unfortunate Nightmare still groaning under the boulder, "...they stay squashed!"

Across the other side of the cavern the distant figure of the Overseer was berating the sorry looking Nightmare who had finally made its way back to where the metal chest had first been dropped and spilled its content. After a brief, heated exchange the pair of them began to load handfuls of the dropped stones back into the container.

"Carter," Maya said, "There is something big going on, and I think they need those stones. I doubt it's for anything good, so it's down to us to stop them."

Carter grimaced, his big, genial features scrunching up as he gave it some thought. "I do wanna help Miss, but that Overseer gives me the proper creeps." While the thought of Carter being afraid of anything seemed ridiculous, (after all Maya could still remember him breaking up a fight down in the docks simply by holding the two participants in the air until they got tired of hitting him), he did seem genuinely scared.

"Tell you what," Maya said reassuringly, patting one of Carters tree-trunk thick arms, "we will go together... okay?"

"Okay then," Carter replied, after a few seconds of thoughtful silence, although he still seemed less than keen on the idea. "Before we go..." He leant down and grabbed the chain that linked the shackles on Maya's wrists. There was a slight grunt of effort and the metal links burst apart, the chains that bound her ankles following suit soon after.

"Thank you," Maya flexed her arms and legs, enjoying the sensation of being able to move freely once again.

"You're welcome Miss"

To Maya's surprise the next thing she felt were the huge fingers of Carter's hand gently grasping hers, completely enveloping it.

"Don't worry Carter. It'll be okay," she told him, giving his hand a reassuring squeeze. It had the same effect as trying to squeeze a pile of bricks, but Carter appeared to appreciate it, and the two of them set out for the far end of the cavern and the distant figure of the Overseer.

As they walked past the nearest group of workers Maya recognised the prisoner who had risked a quick smile in her direction when she had first arrived. He nodded at Maya and got awkwardly to his feet as she passed, shuffling alongside her as fast as his shackles would allow. A moment later he was joined by a couple more prisoners, one an emaciated looking Sornette, the other a Drömer with her facial hair heavily stained with the grime of the Mines.

The same happened with the next group, and the next... and the next, and before Maya knew it, she was at the head of a small, grey, grimly shuffling army. This fact wasn't lost on the Overseer, who had stopped scrabbling around amongst the spilled stones and had turned instead to face them, it's unnaturally large, glowing eyes flicking back and forth across the approaching crowd.

As Maya drew closer, she realised that her first confused impressions of the Overseer had actually been pretty accurate. The squat figure ahead of them was like nothing she had ever seen before. Its arms ended in stubby claws, with long, dark feathers fanning out all the way from the creature's shoulders down to its wrists.

It was also clear why it had spent most of its time perched high above the rest of the cavern, looking down from its eyrie. Despite the continued sense of underlying menace that radiated from the short birdlike creature, it seemed a little awkward and cumbersome down on the ground.

With a cry of anger which rippled across the cavern, echoing back a multitude of times like a discordant choir of rage, the Overseer swung one of its arms in Maya's direction and several of the feathers came loose, flying directly at her and suddenly looking very unpleasant and sharp. Although Maya was quick, the Overseer was so close and it's attack so sudden, that even as she began to dodge to one side, she knew she wouldn't be able to avoid all of the tiny, feathered projectiles. Then her vision was blocked for a moment, and there was a muted, slightly pained grunt.

Carter lowered his arm from where he had raised it to shield Maya and grimaced in concentration as he plucked one of the feathers from the spot where it had lodged itself.

"That was not a very nice thing to do," he said sternly, pulling the last sharp little dart from his arm and then flexing his fingers.

If anything, the anger emanating from the creature facing them only intensified and with a sudden movement of its wings it launched itself into the air, the downward gusts buffeting Maya and her ragtag army. A couple of the bolder prisoners tried heaving small rocks up at the hovering form of the Overseer, but it knocked them to one side dismissively, before launching more of the sharp feathers down at them.

Maya could sense the panic building in her companions, their current bravery and defiance newly born and fragile, and knew she had to do something quickly. She turned to Carter, who was scowling up at the creature above them, still absentmindedly rubbing at his wounded arm.

"Do you think you could get me up there?" Maya asked, nodding at the Overseer.

Carter looked between her and the flying creature, thought for a moment and then nodded.

"Think so miss, might be a bit risky though…"

"Fine," Maya replied, as she backed a few paces away from him, "it can't be any riskier than being pelted with those horrible feathers. You ready?"

Carter nodded again and crouched down into a deep squat, his shovel like hands cupped together in front of him, held close to the ground.

Taking one final deep breath, Maya ran back towards him, planting her right foot in Carter's outstretched hands, and then with a grunt of effort he heaved her skywards, unwinding his whole body and whipping his arms into the air, launching Maya like a catapult.

Maya's perspective shifted violently as she flew into the air, wind rushing past her face, a feeling of sudden and complete freedom surging through her veins. Within moments she was level with the hovering form of the Overseer and without pausing for thought she lashed out with her right arm, the loose chain from Maya's manacle catching the Overseers outstretched wing.

The complete unexpectedness of Maya's sudden attack caught the Overseer completely by surprise and before it could react, they were completely entangled. Within a few seconds both Maya and the Overseer were tumbling back towards the ground in an unruly mess of arms, legs and wings. As they plummeted downwards Maya desperately fought to free her arms and with a final effort she braced her feet against the creature's chest and pushed herself clear, somersaulting back though the air and hoping that somehow she would manage to land without breaking every bone in her body.

They both reached the ground at about the same time, the Overseer's last desperate flap of its wings taking out the very worst of the impact, while Maya was very surprised and relieved to find herself gathered in Carters huge arms rather than clattering into the hard, stony ground as she had expected.

Even with Carter's best efforts to cushion her fall it was still painful, her brain rattling in her head and giving her an instant headache as he caught her, but nothing seemed to be permanently broken and after a couple of seconds Maya felt together enough to lever herself out of Carter's arms and down onto the ground. The squat, winged figure of the Overseer, now looking rather more dishevelled and with one of its wings slightly crumpled and uneven looking, was also staggering upright and there was a long silent pause as Maya and the Overseer weighed each other up, the luminous orbs of its strange eyes giving nothing away.

Then it blinked once, and the spell was broken. It gave a furious shriek, spread its arms wide and with one strong downward stroke shot skywards, leaving behind the dark stones it had been so keen to gather.

The unfortunate Nightmare it had also left behind took one look at Maya and the crowd of prisoners gathered behind her and ran, (or at least limped at speed), away.

Maya looked up, hoping to spot the Overseer, but all she could see was a distant and fading shadow, already too far away to see clearly, high above them all. Then it was gone, presumably vanishing through an opening in the cavern roof.

A tap on her shoulder brought her attention back to their current predicament. Carter pointed to the opening in the cave wall directly ahead of them, making a shushing motion with one large finger.

There was definitely a sound echoing down the corridor beyond the opening, someone or something was coming their way.

Maya signalled to the gathered prisoners to spread out to either side of the cave entrance, just leaving her and Carter standing in the open, although Carter pretty much classed as an army on his own.

The noise of whatever was approaching was growing louder, several pairs of feet pattering across the uneven stone floor.

Maya readied herself, winding the short length of loose chain still dangling from the manacle on her right wrist several times around her fist. To her side Carter also prepared his weapons, essentially by checking that his hands were still on the end of his arms... which to his apparent satisfaction they were. Then the sound of footsteps ended, and several figures stepped out of the corridor into the dim light of the cavern.

CHAPTER 10

The first was tall and well dressed, a fine long-coat and top hat stained with signs of recent battle. To his side a much shorter and unusually attired Drőmer, both of whom Maya recognised from the previous escape.

"You... you..." Maya paused, not really sure what to say.

"I am Augustus Trimble, although some call me the 'Ringmaster'," the taller of two figures said, introducing himself to the gathered prisoners as if it was the most natural thing in the world, "you may have heard of me and my troupe of performers?" He raised one impeccably manicured eyebrow.

Maya was struck by two things, firstly that apparently no one had heard of either Augustus or his companions, with a deafening silence being the only response from the surrounding crowd, and secondly that it was amazing that Augustus had somehow managed to maintain his eyebrows so well, despite being a prisoner in this terrible place.

Not seeming particularly surprised by the lack of response Augustus sighed deeply. "Not to worry, it seems our fame isn't as well travelled as I hoped. Still, that is not the most important thing here."

The small, oddly dressed Drőmer next to him was jigging from side to side with excitement and kept nudging Augustus in the side, apparently keen to move the conversation along.

"Yes, yes... fine," Augustus told his excitable companion, slightly impatiently, "I was getting to that." He turned back to the gathered crowd.

"Something wonderful has happened," he said, his deep, resonant voice flecked with emotion. "The Queen of Nightmares has been defeated... at least for now, by a traveller from the Waking World, a Daydreamer, and his brave companions."

Maya thought back to the sight of Lucid and Grimble sprinting across the cavern, and the boy who had been running with them, and smiled to herself. Whatever else you might think of Lucid and Grimble, if there was trouble to be found you could guarantee they would be drawn to it like a couple of old, bickering moths to a flame.

The Drőmer had stopped his side to side jigging and switched to jumping into the air instead, pumping his fist enthusiastically. "We were there... and it was AMAZING!" he shouted before Augustus shushed him.

"The Nightmares are in disarray," the Ringmaster continued, "for the moment leaderless, and we intend to return here shortly with our vessel, which should be large enough to carry us all back across the Dwam, away from this place. It may take a few days, but if you leave now and head for the coast, we will return and collect you all there. You have my word on that."

A series of excited mutters ran around the cavern, a mixture of happiness and disbelief that there could be some way out of the Mines and its constant, never-ending grind. The Drőmer, who turned out to be called Oomba, which Maya felt rather suited his ridiculously enthusiastic approach to life, wasted no time in working his way around the prisoners, releasing them from their manacles one after another.

The whole group made their way through the winding tunnels of the Mines, stopping briefly in what looked to be some sort of horrible kitchen to gather whatever food they could. The place was abandoned, apparently fairly recently, although Maya oddly found herself hoping that Kreepa had managed to avoid the worst of whatever had taken place, feeling rather sorry for the strange little Nightmare.

They parted ways with Augustus and Oomba when they finally left the network of caves and stepped, blinking into the half-light of the world outside the Mines, promising to meet them at the coast in a few days' time, when the troupe would return with their ship.

CHAPTER 11

The days and nights spent waiting for the ship to arrive passed painfully slowly, each one dragging on much longer than seemed reasonable. The nights were the worst, fitful sleep under makeshift shelters cobbled together from old sheets, shivering in the cold and filled with fears that came with the dark in this place, waiting to see if the Nightmares had returned. There were a couple of times when Maya could have sworn she had seen a distant birdlike silhouette, circling high above them, but each time she squinted into the sky the shape would disappear amongst the shadows of the night, leaving her doubting her eyes.

But on the fourth day, just as their scant supply of food was beginning to run out, there had been a cry from one of the prisoners, a cheerfully optimistic Sornette named Mallett, who had taken it upon herself to watch the horizon each day, staring hungrily into the distance.

"A ship... I see a ship!"

Maya had run to the spot where Mallett was perched and there, far in the distance, but unmistakable, was the silhouette of an approaching ship, a large one.

By the end of the same day, Maya, Carter and the rest of the prisoners were crammed onto the Circus troupe's unusual vessel and had begun their journey home. It was a squeeze, pretty much every square metre of the ship completely full, but no one complained, instead the place was filled with relieved smiles and laughter. Even better than that, Oomba had taken it upon himself to constantly circuit the ship with a trolley loaded with food... proper food that you didn't have to close your eyes and squeeze your nose to eat, and that you could swallow the first time you tried.

As their first day on board the ship drew to close, the gentle glow of the sun covering everything in a soft red glaze, Maya stood with Augustus up on deck, staring out across the never-ending mists of the Dwam.

"I can never thank you enough," she said, "I thought that I would end my days in that terrible place."

"It was the least we could do," the Ringmaster replied, his voice completely serious, without the glossy veneer of showmanship she was used to hearing. "We were saved by the Daydreamer and his friends, and we promised that we would repay that favour by helping others."

Maya nodded silently, having decided to keep her connection to Lucid, Grimble, and the rest of the Five to herself.

"So, any idea what you will do next?" he continued, gesturing across the Dwam to unseen, distant shores. "We head to Nocturne, home for most of our passengers, or at least where they can find a barge to take them on to wherever they want to go." He stopped briefly to check his chart. "We will also pass close to the western fringes of Reverie as we go, but I doubt anyone will be stopping there, it's mainly barren land. I took the troupe there once... pretty tough crowd."

Maya pricked up her ears at the mention of the West and rather than answering the question immediately, she let two possible futures play out in her mind.

In one she returned to Nocturne, to the Five, to the docks and all that came with it. There was adventure and danger, deception and skulduggery. But she also couldn't shake the terrible memory of the

Lady's sorrowful gaze as she closed the door of the Mansion, leaving Maya to her fate, or the thought of Granny's wrinkled, cackling face, watching over the docks like a sociopathic fairy godmother, every wish she granted leaving you stuck even deeper in her pocket.

In the other she visualised the open peaceful spaces of the West and the wreckage of her parent's farm in Perfidy, still waiting out there for someone to raise it back out the ground, to bring it back to life. It would be difficult, back-breaking work, the carnage wrought by the Horror so many years ago incredibly hard to undo, but there was a stubborn resilience deeply ingrained in the land that she knew was still there, waiting to be released.

"You know what," Maya said, a smile working its way in from the edges of her mouth until it met in the middle, forming a broad grin, "I think I know exactly what I am going to do," and dropping back into contended silence she stared out over the mists of the sea and dreamt of the long journey home.

-THE END-

Printed in Great Britain
by Amazon